Miss Dirt
the Dustman's
Daughter

D1148992

Ahlberg & Ross

SWANSEA LIBRARIES

0001422783

PUFFIN BOOKS

UK | USA | Canada | Ireland | Australia
India | New Zealand | South Africa

Puffin Books is part of the Penguin Random House group of companies
whose addresses can be found at global.penguinrandomhouse.com.

www.penguin.co.uk   www.puffin.co.uk   www.ladybird.co.uk

First published in hardback by Viking and in paperback by Puffin Books 1996
This edition published 2016

001

Text copyright © Allan Ahlberg, 1996
Illustrations copyright © Tony Ross, 1996
Educational Advisory Editor: Brian Thompson

The moral right of the author and illustrator has been asserted

Printed in China
A CIP catalogue record for this book is available from the British Library

ISBN: 978–0–141–37486–4

All correspondence to:
Puffin Books, Penguin Random House Children's
80 Strand, London WC2R 0RL

Daisy Dirt was an unusual girl.
She was the poorest
and the richest girl
in the whole town.

Daisy had lots to wear
and nothing to wear;
a huge room of her own
and a tiny room of her own.

She had a little dog

and a big dog,

a little hamster
and a big h . . . .

horse.

A big dinner . . .
and a *very* big dinner!

You see, Daisy lived
half the time with her dad
and half the time with her mum.

Daisy's dad was a dustman.
He was a divorced dustman on the dole.
"What's 'on the dole' mean, Dad?"
said Daisy.
" 'On the dole' means: out of work –
no money – skint!" her dad said.

Daisy's mum was a duchess.
She had got married again – to a duke.
He was a dozy duke in a Daimler.
"What's a 'Daimler', Mum?" said Daisy.

"This is!" said her mum.

Daisy's life was a whirl.
Here is her diary to prove it.

Monday:

breakfast with Dad
school
tea at Betty Biff's
house
home to Mum

Betty

Yes, Daisy's life was a whirl.
She went back and forth
between her mum and dad
like a parcel –
like a pendulum –
like a ping-pong ball.

"I never know if I'm coming
or going," she said.

Then one day Daisy went
to her mum's and found . . .

nothing to wear,
nothing to eat –
and no horse!

There was a crowd in the street;
a car-boot sale on the lawn;
FOR SALE signs everywhere.

You see, the duke
had had some bad luck.
He was stony broke.

"What's 'stony broke' mean, Mum?"
said Daisy.
" 'Stony broke' means: no money – skint!"
"Oh dear!" said Daisy.
"Yes," said her mum.
"I'm a down-and-out duchess."

But still Daisy's life was a whirl.
Still she went back and forth
between her mum and dad
like a homing pigeon
(with *two* homes) –

like a hamster in a wheel.

Here is her diary again to prove it.

Saturday:

breakfast with Mum
jumble sale with Mum
bike ride with Mum
home to Dad

Then one day Daisy went
to her dad's and found . . .

a crowd in the street;
a TV reporter at the door;
photographers everywhere.

You see, Daisy's dad
had had some *good* luck.
He had won the Lottery.

Then out they went for a drive . . .

. . . in a Daimler.

Daisy Dirt was an unusual girl.
She was the richest
and the poorest girl
in the whole town.

And she still is.

The End